TALES OF
AMERICAN INDIANS

RETOLD TIMELESS CLASSICS

Perfection Learning®

Retold by Peg Hall

Editor: Paula Reece
Designer: Jan M. Michalson
Illustrator: Sue F. Cornelison

For information, contact:
Perfection Learning® Corporation
1000 North Second Avenue, P.O. Box 500
Logan, Iowa 51546-0500
Phone: (800) 831-4190 • Fax: (712) 644-2392

Paperback ISBN 0-7891-5065-4
Cover Craft® ISBN 0-7807-9036-7
Printed in the U.S.A.

7 8 9 10 PP 08 07 06 05

Contents

The Girl Who Was the Ring

A Pawnee Legend

Long ago, the men of the Pawnee Indians played many games. Their favorite was a contest played by two men called the stick game. The game tested their speed and how well they could see. It also tested their skill in throwing the stick.

The young men used two tools in this game, a six-inch ring made of buffalo hide and a pair of thin sticks.

This is how the game was played.

Each player got a stick. One young man rolled the ring on smooth ground, and then both players ran after the ring. Each tried to catch the ring on his stick. This was very hard to do because the sticks could knock the ring down.

The players kept track of points. The stick that was closest to the ring would win. But sometimes it was hard to tell which was the winning stick.

In the story below, the game is important. It tells how the Buffalo changed a girl into a ring. Then they used that ring to play the stick game.

Here is the story.

———

There was a lodge on the banks of a river. Four brothers lived in the lodge with their sister.

The brothers hung a leather strap from the branch of a tree. It was a strap like the ones women used to carry wood. But the brothers used the strap as a swing for their sister.

Sometimes the family ran out of meat and got hungry. They then knew it was time to hunt the Buffalo.

Whenever this happened, the sister would send her brothers into the woods. There they would cut thin branches to make arrows. When the brothers came back with the arrows, the sister was always ready.

She would get on the swing, and her brothers would push her back and forth. Before long, they would see dust far off. That is how they knew the Buffalo were coming.

Then the brothers would stand around the swing to keep the Buffalo away from their sister. The Buffalo would run past the swing. As they did, the brothers would shoot at them. They killed many Buffalo this way. Then the other Buffalo would become afraid and would run away.

It always worked this way. And each time, the family always had plenty to eat. They would dry the meat and pile it high in their lodge.

One day, the brothers went off again to make arrows. They left the girl in the lodge by herself. While they were gone, a Coyote came.

The Coyote talked to the girl. He said, "Granddaughter, I am very poor. I have no meat. I am very hungry and so are my children. I told my family I would ask you for food. They laughed at me. They said, 'Your granddaughter will not help you.' "

The girl said, "Grandfather, I have lots of food. The house is full of dried meat. Take what you want. Give it to your children and let them eat."

However, the Coyote started to cry. He said, "My family was right. They said you would not help. They said you would not give me anything. I do not want your dried meat. I want fresh meat. Please help me. If you get on your swing, the Buffalo will come. I do not want a lot of meat. So I will only swing you a little bit. I will use my arrows to keep the Buffalo away from you."

But the girl said, "No, Grandfather. I cannot do this. My brothers are away. I cannot bring the Buffalo without them."

Then the Coyote slapped his chest. "Look at me," he said. "I am strong enough to keep you safe. I can keep the Buffalo away from you. Come on. I will swing you a little. So little that only a few Buffalo will come. You will be safe."

But the girl still said no.

The Coyote asked again and again. At last the girl grew tired of his asking. She told the Coyote that he could swing her a little.

The girl got on the swing, and the Coyote started to push her. At first he gave soft pushes. But then he pushed harder and harder. The swing went high into the air.

The girl cried and tried to get off, but it was too late. The Buffalo were coming. There were many of them coming from all sides.

The Coyote got his arrows ready. He ran around and around the girl on the swing trying to shoot the Buffalo. But there were just too many for him.

Coyote was afraid. He ran into the lodge and left the girl alone. He left her with the Buffalo all around.

One Bull ran under the swing. He put his head up and, at once, the girl was gone!

Then the Coyote looked out the door and saw that the girl was gone. He saw a ring on the horn of the Bull. He knew at once that the ring had to be the girl.

The Bull ran off with all the other Buffalo following.

After that, the Coyote came out of the lodge. He saw the girl was truly gone, and he didn't know what to do.

When the Coyote heard the brothers returning, he was afraid. He knew they had seen the dust. They had to know that someone had been swinging their sister. They had to know that the Buffalo had come.

The brothers ran quickly. When they got to the lodge, they saw the Coyote. He was just getting out of a mud hole. And he was crying.

The Coyote cried, "I tried to save your sister, but the Buffalo ran over me. I did not know so many Buffalo would come. I only pushed the swing a little bit. I thought only a few Buffalo would come."

The brothers were sad that their sister was gone. They talked together about how to get her back.

While the brothers talked, the Coyote stood there. At last he said, "Do not be sad. I will get your sister back. Go on with your lives and do not think about all this. I tell you, I will get her back." Then he said, "Now I am going off on the warpath." And he left.

The Coyote walked alone. He walked a long, long way. After some time, he met a Badger.

The Badger asked, "Where are you going?"

The Coyote said, "I am on the warpath. Will

you come with me?"

The Badger said he would come. So they went on together.

After a long while, they saw a Swift Hawk sitting in a tree. He asked where they were going, and they told him. Then they asked him to come along. The Swift Hawk said he would come.

Later the three travelers met a Kit Fox. He came along too. Then a Jack Rabbit. And then a Blackbird. They all joined Coyote.

After some time, they stopped. That was when Coyote told his story. He told them about how the girl had been lost. He told them that he had to get her back, and he told them about his plan.

The others listened. They said they would help.

Soon they were ready to move again. They stood up and got ready to go, but the Coyote spoke to the Blackbird. "Friend, I want you to stay here. Stay until the time comes."

So the Blackbird stayed. The others went on with the Coyote.

In a little while, they stopped again. This time Coyote spoke to the Hawk. He asked him to stay and wait.

So the Hawk stayed behind while the others went on.

Next he asked the Rabbit to stay. Then the Kit Fox. And last of all, the Badger. They all stayed where the Coyote told them to.

The Coyote walked on alone a long, long way. Early one day, he came to the Buffalo camp. He went to the place where the young Bulls liked to play the stick game. The Coyote lay down there.

After some time, the young Bulls came. They started to roll the ring. They threw sticks at it.

Now, the Coyote knew that the ring was the girl. And he knew that he had to get her back.

The Coyote stood up. His hair was covered with mud. His mouth hung open. He fell down on the ground and cried. He looked very, very sick. This was his first plan to get back the ring.

The young Bulls did not look at the Coyote. Not until he got up and staggered over to the ring. Then they called out, "Do not get in the way!"

Coyote realized that this plan would not allow him to get the ring. So Coyote came up with another plan. After a time, the Coyote acted like he felt better. He went over to watch the game. He sat down with some other Bulls who were watching too.

Sometimes two of the players would start to fight. One would say that his stick was closer to the ring. Another would say his was closer.

Finally the Coyote went up to two of the Bulls. He said, "You do not need to fight about this. Let me look. I know all about this game. I can tell which stick is closer."

The Bulls stopped fighting. One said, "Let him look."

Another said, "Let us hear what he says."

The Coyote went up to the ring. He looked at one stick, then at the other. "That stick is closer," he said at last.

The Bulls looked at each other. They nodded and said, "He is right. He knows."

Then they went on with the game. Once, they asked the Coyote to look again. Again he told them which stick was closer.

At last two of the Bulls got into a great fight. The Coyote was called over to settle things. "This is very close," he said. "So I must look carefully. But I need some room. You must all stand back. Go over to that hill. Sit down there and wait."

The Bulls wanted the argument settled. So they went to the hill and sat down to wait.

The Coyote went to one stick and looked at it carefully. He went to the other stick and looked again. He acted like he could not make up his mind. He went back and forth. He even got down on the ground to look.

Then the Coyote grabbed the ring! He ran away as fast as he could.

The Bulls did not want to lose the ring. At once they started running after him.

The Coyote ran very fast. At first he was ahead, but he got tired and started to slow down. The Buffalo were catching up to him. They were going to run right over him!

Then the Coyote reached the top of a great hill. On the other side was the Badger, sitting near a hole.

The Coyote raced down the hill and gave the ring to the Badger. At once they both jumped into the hole.

The Buffalo ran to the hole. For a time, they stood around it. Then they tried to dig it up. But the Badger had dug a good hole. It went under the ground for a long way and came back up in another place.

So the Buffalo continued trying to dig up the hole. And the Badger ran out of the other end of the hole. He raced toward the riverbank to find the brothers' lodge.

But the Buffalo saw him go. They shouted, "There he is! Get him!"

The Buffalo got close to the Badger. But before they could catch him, he dug another hole. He went under the ground and came out in another spot far away. Then he started to run again.

Before long, the Buffalo spotted the Badger. Once more, they began to chase after him.

Badger did this again and again, but soon he got tired. He knew he could not run much longer. He could not keep digging holes.

Then the Badger saw the Kit Fox. The Fox was lying on a rock and sleeping in the sun.

The Badger called, "Brother Fox! Help me! I am tired!"

The Kit Fox jumped up and took the ring from the Badger. Then he ran off. The Badger dug a deep hole and hid there.

The Fox ran fast like a bird. Still the Buffalo saw him and set off after him.

The Fox stayed ahead of the Buffalo for a long time. But at last he got tired. He came to where the Rabbit was waiting. He gave the ring to the Rabbit, and he hid in a hole.

Rabbit ran on with the Buffalo following him. They almost caught up, but Rabbit came to where the Swift Hawk was waiting.

The Hawk took the ring in his claws and flew off. Rabbit went to hide in the long grass.

The Buffalo ran after the Hawk. They never seemed to get tired! But the Hawk did get tired. He flew lower and lower. He was hardly able to stay above the Buffalo.

At last the Hawk reached the Blackbird. The Blackbird had heard the pounding of feet. He knew the Buffalo were coming, so he had flown up on a sunflower stem and waited there.

As the Buffalo ran past, the Blackbird flew to the Hawk. He took the ring and slipped it around his neck.

The ring was heavy, and the Blackbird was a small bird. He couldn't stay in the air, and he needed to rest. So he landed on the back of one of the Buffalo. Then he moved onto the back of another Buffalo.

The Buffalo tossed their heads. They tried to hit the Blackbird with their horns. They even pushed one another to get to him.

Soon the Buffalo went over a hill. They had almost reached the brothers' lodge. And still they had not been able to get the Blackbird.

Now the Blackbird flew off a Buffalo's back. He flew inside the lodge with the ring still around his neck.

The brothers were ready for the Buffalo. They had been making arrows while their sister was gone. Now they had piles of arrows near their lodge.

When they saw the Buffalo, the brothers got their bows. They shot and shot. They killed many, many Buffalo. The ones they didn't kill ran away in fear.

At last the brothers went into their lodge. There they saw a girl sitting by the fire. It was their sister!

Old Man and the Roasted Squirrels
A Blackfeet Legend

One day Old Man was walking. He came to a place where many squirrels were playing in hot ashes.

Old Man watched. Some squirrels lay down in the hot ashes, and other squirrels covered them with more ashes. When it got too hot, the squirrels would cry out. Then their brother squirrels would dig them out.

After a while, Old Man asked if he could play too.

The squirrels said yes. So Old Man asked, "May I be baked first?"

"Oh no," said the squirrels. "You do not know how to play. You could get burned. We will go first. Then you can see how to play."

Old Man asked again. Still, the squirrels said he could not be first.

At last Old Man gave in. But he said, "There are so many of you. Let me cover all of you at once. That will save some time."

The squirrels agreed. Except for one squirrel who was soon to be a mother. She asked him not to put her in the ashes. Old Man felt sorry for her. "Well, go ahead. Run away," he said. "So there may be other squirrels."

Old Man then tended to the other squirrels. He covered all of the squirrels with ashes. Before long some of them got very hot. "Take us out!" they cried.

Instead, Old Man put on more ashes. The squirrels were soon roasted.

Then Old Man took some branches from a red willow. He used them to make a table. When he was done, he put the roasted squirrels on the table. (The squirrel meat made the branches greasy. And that is why even now the red willow tree feels greasy.)

The Old Man ate many squirrels. He ate and ate until he was full. Then he lay down and went to sleep beside a tree.

Along came Lynx. He saw the roasted squirrels. And he licked his lips.

Lynx looked around to see who the roasted squirrels belonged to. That's when he saw the sleeping Old Man. Slyly, Lynx ate. He ate and ate until he had eaten all the squirrels that were left on the table. Then he quickly ran off.

Soon Old Man woke up. Sleeping had made him hungry again. So he went to the table to finish off his squirrels. That's when he noticed that his table was empty. "My roasted meat is gone!" he cried.

So Old Man looked around, trying to find any clues to his missing meat. That's when he spied the tracks made by Lynx. Old Man decided to follow them.

Now, Lynx was fast. He ran and ran, far away from Old Man. But Lynx had just finished off a big meal. So he, too, became sleepy. He lay down under a tree for a nap.

Old Man kept following the tracks. He wasn't as fast as Lynx, but he wouldn't give up. He kept walking. The longer he walked, the madder he got. He couldn't wait to catch up to the squirrel thief.

Finally, Old Man found Lynx asleep under a tree.

Old Man was mad. He was very mad. He was so mad that he grabbed Lynx by the ears and banged his head into a rock. This made his head shorter.

But Old Man was still mad. So he pulled off Lynx's tail and broke it in two.

But the anger still hadn't left Old Man. So next he grabbed the bushy part of Lynx's tail. Then he stuck that bushy half onto Lynx's hind end.

But Old Man was not done. He was calmer. But he was still a little angry. What else could he do to Lynx?

After a moment of thought, Old Man decided to pull on Lynx's body.

Old Man still had a little fire left in him. So next he stretched out Lynx's legs. Soon they were long and thin.

Finally Old Man was done. His anger was gone.

Old Man threw Lynx to the ground. He studied how Lynx now looked.

Then Old Man said, "You are no longer a Lynx. You are a bobcat now. You will always have a bobtail. You will always be too skinny to run far."

Lynx, now Bobcat, took off running. But he wasn't as fast as before.

Old Man could no longer feel his anger. But now he could feel something on his hands.

Old Man looked at his hands to see what was bothering him. That's when he saw that the hot ashes had burned his hands.

His hands felt like they were still on fire. Old Man looked around. He needed to find something to cool his red palms.

Just then he felt a little breeze across his face. That gave him an idea.

Old Man called out to the Wind, "Blow!"

The Wind blew and blew. The cool air felt good on his burnt hands.

"Blow harder!" Old Man called. The Wind was afraid of Old Man. It had seen what he had done to Lynx. So the Wind blew harder.

Again Old Man told the Wind to blow even harder. He did this again and again. And each time the Wind blew harder.

Soon the Wind was wild. It picked up Old Man and blew him far, far away.

At first Old Man was frightened. He had never flown through the air like this. He grabbed at trees. But every tree he grabbed pulled out of the ground.

And still the Wind blew him.

At last Old Man grabbed a birch tree. But he did not pull up this tree by its roots. The birch tree held fast to the ground. And Old Man held fast to it.

At last the Wind ran out of energy. It had blown so hard that it became tired. So it died down.

Just as the Wind died down, Old Man was no longer afraid of being blown around. In fact, he realized that he was having fun.

So Old Man became angry again. He spoke angrily to the birch tree. "Why are your roots so strong? Why is it that I cannot pull you up? I was having a good time. The Wind was blowing me all over until you stopped me."

The Old Man was mad at the birch tree. He wished he were still flying in the air.

That's when he took out his knife. And he cut the bark of the birch tree into long strips.

Soon Old Man was no longer angry.

He looked at the birch tree. It looked beat up.

And that is the way birch trees look to this day.

WHERE ILLNESS and MEDICINE COME FROM
A Cherokee Myth

In the old days, the animals and plants could talk. They lived together with the People in peace, and they were all friends.

But as time went by, there were more and more People. Soon they were everywhere on the earth. The animals began to run out of room.

Then things got worse. The People made bows and arrows, knives, and spears. They began to kill large animals for their skins and flesh. They stepped on small animals without thinking.

So the animals got together to talk. They had to find a way to be safe from the People.

The Bears were the first. They met in their home under the great mountain. The Old White Bear Chief led the meeting.

Each Bear had a turn to talk. Each told of how the People killed its friends. How the People ate the Bear's flesh and wore its skin for clothing.

The Bears decided to go to war against the People.

Then one Bear asked, "What tools do the People use to fight us?"

The other Bears spoke as one. "Bows and arrows, of course."

"What are these made of?" asked the first Bear.

Only one Bear spoke now. It said, "The bow is made of wood. Its string is made from our guts."

The Bears wanted to see if they could use the same tools. They wanted to fight man with bows and arrows.

But first they had to make the bows and arrows. So one Bear got a piece of locust wood for the bow. Another Bear gave its life to make the strings. It did this for all the Bears because it was their brother.

Soon everything was done. The Bears went to test their bows and arrows. The first bear shot an arrow. But its claws got in the way of the string, and the arrow did not fly.

One Bear said, "Cut your claws. Then they will not get in the way."

The Bear did that. The next time it shot an arrow, it hit its mark.

But now the Old White Bear was upset. It said, "Bears must have long claws so they can climb trees. One Bear has already given its life for us. Now you say we must all cut our claws. If we do that, we will die. Forget about the People's tools. Instead, let us keep our claws and our teeth. These are the tools we must use against the People."

No one could think of a better plan. So the Old Chief sent the Bears away.

The Bears went to the woods and to the bushes. But unfortunately, they still had no way to fight man.

What if the Bears had done something else? Then we would be at war with them. But now the hunter does not talk to the Bear. He does not ask if he may kill the Bear. He just does it.

The Deer met next. They talked for some time. At last they came up with a plan. The Deer knew that the People needed to hunt. That was how they got their food. But the Deer wanted hunters to ask for forgiveness before killing them. If the hunter did not, an illness would be sent to him.

So the Deer sent word to the Indian camp. They told the Indians what to do. This is what they said.

"Sometimes you must kill a Deer. We know this. But the Deer runs fast and its spirit cannot be hurt by your arrows.

"If you shoot a Deer, it will bleed. So go to the spot where the Deer was shot. Bend down there and ask the spirit of the Deer for forgiveness. The Deer may say yes. Then all will be well.

"But the Deer may say no. Then its spirit will follow the hunter. It will follow the drops of blood on the ground until it comes to the hunter's cabin. It will go inside and make the hunter sick. So sick that he will not be able to hunt again."

That is why hunters always talk to the spirit of the Deer. They ask it to forgive them for killing it. (Some hunters have not learned this. They try to turn away the spirit of the Deer by making a fire on the path.)

Next came the Fish and Reptiles. They, too, were angry at the People. They met together and came up with a plan. They would give the People terrible dreams. Dreams of snakes twisting around them. Dreams of evil smells blowing in their faces. Dreams of eating rotten fish and dying. This is why today the People dream terrible dreams about snakes and fish.

———

Last were the Birds, Insects, and smaller animals. They met for the same reason. The Grubworm led the others. It said that every one of them would get a chance to talk. Then they would vote. They would decide if they should punish the People. If seven animals voted yes, it would happen.

One after another they talked. They all spoke of the People's unkindness to animals. And they all voted to punish the People.

The Frog was first. "There are too many People," he said. "We must get rid of them, or soon they will fill the earth. There will be no room for us. See how they treat me. They say I am ugly and they kick me. That is why my back looks like this." And he showed them his spots.

Next came the Bird. No one remembers which Bird it was. It voted to punish the People as well. "People burn my feet off!" it cried. It was talking about how the People cooked Birds. They would put the Bird on a stick. Then they would hang the stick over a fire until the Bird's feathers and feet burned away.

Other animals spoke in the same way. None of them had anything good to say about the People, except for the small Ground Squirrel. He alone had something good to say. This made the other animals angry. They fell upon the Ground Squirrel and tore his back with their claws. This is why the Ground Squirrel now has stripes.

———

At last all the animals had talked. And every one of them (except the Ground Squirrel) spoke against the People. So the animals made up many kinds of sickness. They named each one. It was a good thing they finally ran out of ideas. Otherwise, there would be no People left on earth.

The animals were pleased with their work. The Grubworm was the happiest of all. "The People step on me," it said. "I am glad that they will die of sickness!" It began to shake with joy. So much so that it fell over on its back and couldn't get to its feet again. And to this day the Grubworm has to wiggle along the ground on its back.

———

Soon the Plants heard the news about what the animals were doing. But the Plants were friendly to the People. They wanted to do something to help. Every Tree and Bush wanted to help. Every Herb, Moss, and Grass felt the same.

The Plants all spoke. Each said, "I will come to the People when they call. I will come when they need me."

———

This is how medicine came to the earth. Every Plant can fight sickness. We just need to know how to use each one. Even weeds have good uses. We must find this out for ourselves. Sometimes a doctor comes to a sick person. The doctor may not know what Plant to use, but the spirit of the Plant will tell him. He only has to listen.

The Legend of Onarga
An Iroquois Legend

Campfires lit the forest like stars in the sky. Great oak trees grew all around. It was the time of the Harvest Moon.

The Great Spirit had been kind to the Iroquois, and they were happy. The crop of corn was large. Many buffalo ran across the open plains, and the streams were filled with fish.

Their chief sat at the door of his wigwam. His daughter sat at his side. Her name was Onarga. She was the most beautiful girl in the land.

Together they looked out at the corn. Its leaves moved in the wind. They looked out at the moonlight. It made its way through the trees and danced on the thick grass.

Onarga had a question. "Father, why does the North Wind blow so? Why does it move through the corn and the leaves of the trees?"

Her father said, "The Great Spirit has been kind. He sent you to the Iroquois people. Where you step, the grass grows green. Where you are, the buffalo stay close by. They know there will be food for them. Your touch helps the corn grow. So there is food for our people. When you sing, the birds sing with you. When you speak, the rivers laugh with joy to hear your voice. The Great Spirit smiles and is glad.

"You are the Fairest Daughter of the Morning. What you hear is not really the wind. It is the sound of many waters. It is the dipping of paddles. It is the sound of the Great Canoe. The Great Canoe is coming, my daughter."

The next morning, the Sun God rose above the trees. But now there was sadness in the camp. In the night, Onarga had gone to the Great Canoe. She had gone to the happy Hunting Grounds of the Iroquois. To the home of the White Rabbit.

Each year the Harvest Moon shines on the grassy plains of the Iroquois. The plains are bright with its light. And each year the Great Canoe sails on the mist. The spirits of brave Iroquois paddle the canoe. It floats on the North Wind and then returns to the faraway hunting grounds. To the happy Hunting Grounds of the Iroquois.

Some say they have seen the Great Canoe. They say a beautiful Indian girl sits in it. She lifts her hand to Heaven and blesses the Iroquois people.

Each season the Harvest Moon shines between two great trees. That is where Onarga sleeps. It is quiet by her grave. But they say shadow and moonlight still play there. Once the Iroquois campfires burned in that spot. Now it is the Village of Onarga.

Coyote Dances with a Star
A Cheyenne Trickster Tale

The Great Mystery gave much of his medicine to Coyote. So Coyote was very powerful. That is why Coyote thought a lot of himself. He thought he could do anything. He even thought he was more powerful than the Great Mystery. Coyote was sometimes wise, but he was also a fool.

One day long ago, something came into Coyote's mind. He wanted to dance with a star. "I really feel like doing this," Coyote said.

He saw a bright star in the sky. The star hung high above a mountain. Coyote called out, "Star! Come down! I want to dance with you!"

The star came down. Soon it was so low that Coyote could reach it. He grabbed hold. At once the star shot back up in the sky, and Coyote hung on for dear life.

Round and round the sky went the star. Coyote soon got very tired. The arm that was holding the star started to hurt. Coyote felt as if it were going to fall off.

"Star," he called. "I am done. That is enough dancing for me. I will let go now. I must be getting home."

The star answered, "No. We are too high. Wait until we are lower. Wait until I get back to the spot where I picked you up."

Coyote looked down at the earth. He thought it looked very near. "I am tired, Star," he said. "I think I will leave now. We are low enough." So he let go of the star.

But Coyote had made a big mistake. He dropped down, down, down. He fell for a full ten winters.

At last he fell through the clouds that covered the earth. When he hit the ground, he was flattened. He looked like a deerskin stretched out for tanning. So Coyote died right there and then.

Now Coyote was lucky. The Great Mystery had given him more than one life. Even so, it took Coyote a few winters to puff himself up again. At last he was back to his old shape.

Coyote had grown older in all that time. But he had not grown wiser. He bragged, saying, "Who else could do this? Who else could dance with the stars? And then fall from the sky for ten winters. Who else could be flattened out like a deer hide? And yet live to tell the tale. I am Coyote. I am powerful. I can do anything!"

Coyote was sitting in front of his lodge one night. A strange star rose over the mountain. It was a fast star with a long tail trailing along behind it.

Coyote said to himself, "Look at that fast star. What fun it would be to dance with him!" He called out, "Star! Star with the long tail! Wait for me! Come down here! Let's dance!"

The strange, fast star shot down. Coyote grabbed hold of it. The star sped off into the great darkness of space.

Again, Coyote had made a big mistake. He had no idea how fast the strange star really was. It was the fastest thing in all the world. It spun Coyote around and around. First one leg dropped off. Then the other. Bit by bit, small pieces of Coyote were torn off. At last only Coyote's hand was left. It held onto the fast star.

All the pieces of Coyote fell to earth. A bit here and a bit there. But soon the pieces started looking for one another. Slowly they came together. And slowly Coyote was formed again. It took a long time—much more than one winter. But at last Coyote was whole again. Except for his right hand. That was still speeding through space with the star.

Coyote cried out. "Great Mystery! I was wrong. I am not as powerful as you are. I am not as powerful as I thought I was. Have pity on me!"

Then the Great Mystery spoke. "Friend Coyote. I have given you four lives. You have already lost two of them. Better be careful!"

Again Coyote cried out. "Great Mystery! Have pity on me. Give me back my right hand!"

"That is not up to me," said the Great Mystery. "It is up to the star with the long tail. You must wait until you see the star again. Until it rises from behind the mountain once more. Then maybe it will give your hand back."

"How long must I wait?" asked Coyote. "How often does the star come over the mountain?"

"Once in a hundred lifetimes," said the Great Mystery.

How Saynday Got the Sun

A Kiowa Legend

One day, Saynday was walking along. All the world around him was dark. It was as black as midnight. There was no sun on this side of the world. The sun belonged to people who lived on the other side. And they always kept it near them so no one could take it.

As Saynday was walking along, he met some of the animals. They were Fox, Deer, and Magpie. The three were sitting together by a prairie dog hole, talking about things.

"What is the matter?" asked Saynday.

"We do not like this world," said Fox.

"And what is wrong with it?" asked Saynday.

"We do not like all this dark," said Deer.

"What is wrong with the darkness?" asked Saynday.

"Things cannot live and grow. Things cannot be happy," said Magpie.

"Then we should do something about it," said Saynday.

So the four of them sat by the prairie dog hole. They thought and thought and thought and thought. They were so quiet that the Prairie Dog came out to look. He stayed there with them. And he joined them in thought.

"There is a sun," said Saynday at last.

"Where is it?" asked Fox.

"On the other side of the world," said Saynday.

"What is it doing there?" asked Deer.

"The people who have it will not let it go," said Saynday.

"That means it is no good to us," said Magpie.

"Then we should do something about it," said Saynday.

So they sat a while longer. They thought and thought and thought and thought some more.

None of them moved at all.

At last Saynday said, "We could go and take the sun for a while."

"That would not really be stealing," said Fox.

"We do not want keep it," said Saynday.

"We can give it back sometimes," said Deer.

"Then things could live and grow there," said Magpie.

"But they could live and grow here too," added Saynday.

Then Saynday got busy. His thinking was done and now he could work.

"How far can you run?" he asked Fox.

"A long, long way," said Fox.

"How far can you run?" he asked Deer.

"A short long way," said Deer.

"How far can you run?" he asked Magpie.

"A long short way," said Magpie.

"I cannot run very far," said Saynday. "So I will have to be last."

Then he lined them all up. He told them what to do. Fox was to go to the village on the other side of the world. He would make friends with the people there. That was the first thing to do. It was also the hardest.

So Fox left. For a long time, he ran in the dark. Then he saw a thin line of light at the edge of the world. As Fox ran toward the light, it got brighter and brighter. Soon it was a great ball of light that filled the sky.

Fox ran to the top of a hill. Below him was the village where the people with the sun lived. So Fox sat down and watched them. He thought about what he should do.

The people were playing a game with the sun. They stood in two rows. Each side had four spears. They rolled the sun along the ground like a ball. Then they threw spears at it. The side that hit the most times won. One side was far ahead of the other.

Fox went down the hill. He lay on the ground and watched the game. The people rolled the sun. The side that was ahead won again. So Fox said something very quietly. Only the captain of the losing side could hear. Fox said, "Good luck to the losers."

The captain looked at Fox. But he didn't say anything. The people rolled the sun again. And this time the losing side won. The captain came over to Fox. "Thank you for wishing us well," he said.

"Good luck to your winning," said Fox. And the losing side won again.

The men on the other side wanted Fox to go away. The side that had been losing wanted Fox to stay. The two sides had a fight. But Fox's side won, and he was able to stay.

Fox stayed and stayed and stayed in the village. He stayed until he knew it better than his own home. He stayed until he knew all the people. He knew what they did and where they lived. He stayed until he knew where they kept the sun. And until he knew the men who kept watch over it. He stayed until he knew the rules of the game they played. He even played the game with them. And all the time, he was making a plan.

One day there was a big game to decide the winners for the year. Fox was playing too. He was on the side he had wished luck. Everyone else rolled the sun before Fox. At last it was Fox's turn. He took the sun in his paws. He bent over as if he were going to roll it. But instead, he started to run. He ran off with the sun!

The people were surprised. At first, they didn't know what to do. Then they got mad and started after Fox. But Fox was a fast runner. He could go a long, long way. That was why Saynday had put him first. So Fox ran all the way to Deer.

Deer didn't even look at the sun. He took it from Fox and started running. He ran and ran. He ran until he was almost ready to give up. But then he saw Magpie.

By now the village people were far behind. They couldn't even be seen. But Magpie took no chances. He grabbed the sun from Deer and started to run. He ran as fast and as far as he could. Just when he was about to give up, Magpie saw Saynday. He gave the sun to him.

The sun people were far, far behind now. Saynday didn't even have to run. He put the sun over his shoulder like a sack of meat and walked along slowly. His friends were able to catch up with him. Soon they got back to the prairie dog hole. They all sat down to rest.

"Well, now we have the sun," said Saynday.

"Now we have light," said Fox.

"Now we can see what we are doing and where we are going," said Saynday.

"Now we can travel around," said Deer.

"Now plants can grow," said Saynday.

"Now there will be trees to live in," said Magpie.

"We brought light to the world," said Saynday.

But there was TOO much light! Before, it had been dark all the time. Now it was light all the time. People could travel, but they got tired because they never had to stop. The plants and trees could grow, but they never stopped growing. One night Magpie and his wife went to bed in a tree that was ten feet off the ground. When they woke up, the tree was 20 feet tall. Everyone started to get mad.

At last the three friends went to see Saynday. He was sitting in front of his lodge, looking at the sun.

"What is the matter?" he asked.

"There is too much light," said Fox.

"We do not want so much," added Deer.

"We do not NEED so much!" said Magpie.

"What can we do?" asked Saynday.

"We could put the sun somewhere else," said Fox.

"That is a good idea," said Saynday.

He put the sun in his lodge. But the light came right through the walls.

"Put it up off the ground," said Deer.

"All right," said Saynday. He put the sun on the very top of his lodge. Poof! It burned the lodge down!

"Throw it away!" said Magpie.

"All right," said Saynday. "I do not want the old thing."

He threw it up into the sky, and there it hung.

They all stared at the sun in its new home.

"That is a good place for it," said Fox.

"It is too far away to burn things," said Saynday.

"It has lots of room to move around," said Deer.

"It can move from one end of the world to the other," said Saynday.

"Now things can grow a little at a time," said Magpie.

"Now the people can share the light," said Saynday. "Here and on the other side of the world."

And that's the way it was. And that's the way it is, to this day.

The Play

How Saynday Got the Sun

A Kiowa Legend

Cast of Characters

Storyteller

Saynday

Fox

Deer

Magpie

The Sun People:

    Captain

    Player

Act One

Storyteller: Long ago, one side of the world was always dark. There was no sun, so the world was as black as midnight. The sun belonged to those who lived on the other side. They were called the Sun People. They always kept the sun nearby. They didn't want anyone to take it away from them.

Saynday lived on the dark side of the world. One day he stopped to talk to Fox, Deer, and Magpie. They sat together by a prairie dog hole.

Saynday: What's the matter, my friends?

Fox: We don't like this world.

Saynday: And what is wrong with it?

Deer: We don't like all this dark.

Saynday: Now, what's wrong with the dark?

Magpie: Things can't live in the dark. They can't grow and be happy.

Saynday: Well, I guess we should do something about it then.

Storyteller: The four of them sat by the prairie dog hole. They thought and thought and thought and thought. They were so quiet that Prairie Dog began to wonder. He stuck his head out of his hole. He saw them thinking and thinking. So he began to think too.

Saynday: You know, there is a sun.

Fox: Where is it?

Saynday: On the other side of the world.

Deer: What is it doing way over there?

Saynday: The Sun People won't let it go.

Magpie: Then what use is it to us?

Saynday: Not any. So I guess we'd better do something about it.

Storyteller: So again they sat. They thought and sat. They sat and thought some more. None of them moved.

Saynday: We could go and borrow the sun.

Fox: It wouldn't really be stealing.

Saynday: You are right. We don't want to keep it forever.

Deer: We would give it back to them sometimes.

Magpie: Then things could live and grow on their side of the world.

Fox: But they would live and grow here too.

Saynday: Our thinking is done. Now we must *do* something. How far can you run, Fox?

Fox: A long, long way.

Saynday: How far can you run, Deer?

Deer: A short long way.

Saynday: How far can you run, Magpie?

Magpie: A long short way.

Saynday: I can't run very far myself. So I guess I will be the last runner. Fox, you will be the first. Run to the other side of the earth. Make friends with the Sun People. That is the first thing we must do. It is also the hardest.

Fox: I will go now.

Act Two

Storyteller: Fox ran a long, long way in the dark. At last he saw a thin line of light at the edge of the world. As he ran, the light got brighter and brighter. Soon it filled the sky ahead of him. Then he was on a hill, and below him was the village of the Sun People. Fox sat down to watch and think.

Fox: I see that the people are playing a game with the sun. They are rolling it along the ground like a big ball. They are taking turns throwing their spears at it. It must be that the side that hits the sun the most wins. And I can see that one side is way ahead of the other.

Storyteller: His thinking done, Fox went down into the village. He lay on the ground with his nose on his paws. He watched the people play. They rolled the sun again. The side that was ahead won even more points. The other side lost again. At last Fox spoke softly.

Fox: Good luck to the losers.

Storyteller: Only the captain of the losing side could hear Fox. He turned his head for a minute. Then the sun was rolled along the ground again. But this time the losing side won. Their captain came over to Fox.

Captain: Thank you for wishing us well.

Fox: Good luck to your winning.

Storyteller: The captain went back to play the game. And his side won again. Some of the Sun People were angry.

Player: Our side was winning. Now it is not. Send Fox away from here.

Captain: No. We want him to stay. He brings our side luck.

Storyteller: They went back and forth this way for some time. But Fox's side was the strongest. So he was able to stay. He stayed and stayed and stayed in that village. He stayed until he knew all the people by name. He knew what they did and where they lived. He stayed until he found out who had the sun when they weren't playing. He stayed until he knew all the rules of the game. He even played the game himself. And all this time, he was making a plan.

Act Three

Storyteller: It was time for the biggest game of the year. The game that would decide who was champion.

Captain: Fox, you will play on our side. Ever since you wished us luck, we have been winning. But you must wait your turn to play. We will all roll the sun first because we were playing first. Then you will roll.

Fox: I will wait.

Storyteller: The game went on for a long time. At last it was Fox's turn to roll the sun. He took the sun in his paws. This was how the people had taught him. He bent over as if he were going to roll the sun. But instead of rolling, he started running.

Player: What is Fox doing?

Captain: He is taking the sun! Stop him!

Player: Catch him! Catch Fox!

Storyteller: The Sun People ran after Fox. But he was fast and could run a long, long way. That is why Saynday had put him first. He ran and ran, and at last he caught up to Deer.

Deer: Give me the sun! I will run with it now!

Fox: Hurry, my friend! The Sun People are coming!

Storyteller: So Deer ran and ran. He ran until he was tired. Then he caught up with Magpie.

Magpie: Give me the sun! I will run with it now!

Deer: Hurry! I cannot see the Sun People anymore. But they are coming!

Magpie: I will hurry. I won't take any chances.

Storyteller: Magpie ran as fast and as far as he could. Just when his breath was gone, he came to Saynday.

Magpie: Here is the sun. Hurry!

Saynday: The Sun People are far behind now, my friend. They cannot catch us now, so I don't need to run. I can walk.

Storyteller: So Saynday put the sun over his shoulder. He walked along so slowly that his friends caught up with him. Soon they were back at their old prairie dog hole. They sat down to rest.

Act Four

Saynday: Well, now we have the sun.

Fox: Now we have light.

Saynday: Now we can see what we're doing. And where we're going.

Deer: Now we can travel around.

Saynday: Now plants will come out of the ground and grow.

Magpie: Now there will be trees to live in.

Saynday: I guess we brought light to the world.

Storyteller: But soon there was trouble. There was too much light! Before it had been dark all the time. Now it was light all the time. People could travel around. But they never stopped traveling, so they got tired. Plants and trees could grow, but they never stopped growing. Magpie and his wife went to bed in a tree ten feet off the ground. They woke up in a tree 20 feet off the ground. Magpie was very unhappy. He got the others, and they went to see Saynday.

The Play: How Saynday Got the Sun: A Kiowa Legend

Saynday: What is the matter, my friends?

Fox: There's too much light.

Deer: We don't want so much.

Magpie: We don't NEED so much.

Saynday: What can we do?

Fox: We could try putting the sun somewhere else.

Saynday: That's a good idea. Here, let's take it to my lodge.

Storyteller: So Saynday put the sun inside his lodge. But its light shone through the walls.

Deer: Let's try putting it up off the ground.

Saynday: All right. I will put it on the very top of my lodge.

Storyteller: So Saynday put the sun on top of his lodge. Whoosh! It burned the lodge to the ground.

Magpie: I think we should throw the sun away!

Saynday: All right. I don't want the old thing. I

will throw it up into the sky. Just like this.

Fox: There it goes! That's a good place for it, actually.

Saynday: It's far enough away not to burn things.

Deer: It has plenty of room to move around.

Saynday: It can move from one side of the world to the other.

Magpie: So things can grow a little bit at a time.

Saynday: And all the people of the world can share its light.

Storyteller: And that's the way it was. It is still that way to this day.